A Mummy for Owen

SIMON AND SCHUSTER

First published in Great Britain in 2007 by Simon & Schuster UK Ltd
1st floor, 222 Gray's Inn Road, London WC1X 8HB

Originally published in the USA by Simon & Schuster Books for Young Readers, 2007

The text for this book is set in Requiem
The illustrations are rendered in acrylic paint and coloured pencils

A CIP catalogue record for this book is available from the British Library upon request

ISBN-13 978-1-8473-8095-1

Printed in China
3 5 7 9 10 8 6 4 2

A Mummy for Owen

By Marion Dane Bauer
Illustrated by John Butler

Owen was a very young hippo.

He lived with his mother, his father, his aunts,
and his cousins in the Sabaki River in Africa.

Owen loved the river.
But even more he loved his great greyish brown – or was
she brownish grey? – mummy.
Every day Owen and his mummy slept together.
They swam together. They ate together.
Even when Mummy left the river to graze in the moonlight,
Owen followed close behind her stubby tail.

Best of all, Owen loved to play hide-and-seek.

Mummy hid and Owen found her.

And every time he found his mummy,
he licked her friendly face,
laid his head on her broad back,
and smiled his great pink smile.

But all that was before
the rain began to fall.

The rain fell
and it fell
and it fell.
The Sabaki River rose
and it rose
and it rose.
The river ran faster
and faster
and faster.
The river rose so high
and ran so fast
that it washed
Owen
and his mother
and his father
and his aunts
and his cousins
all the way out to sea.

Owen roared for his mummy,
but she did not answer.
He roared louder. No Mummy!
He searched and searched,
but his mummy wasn't hiding.
She was lost.
And Owen was alone in the sea.

He roared
and roared
and roared
until finally he
lost even his roar.

And that was when the great wave came
and washed Owen back to shore.

Owen was befuddled and weak and very, very sad.
He looked all around this new place. This wasn't his river!
He looked around some more. Where was his mummy?

Then Owen saw… something brownish grey.

Or was it greyish brown?

He wasn't sure.

But he staggered over and
snuggled down next to it.

And the very old tortoise, whose name was Mzee,
lay very still while Owen waited for sleep to come.

When Owen woke, he looked again at the tortoise.
Mzee was coloured just like his mummy.
Mzee was large just like his mummy.
Mzee had stayed very close when Owen needed
just like his mummy used to do.

Owen laid his head on Mzee's broad back
and slept again.

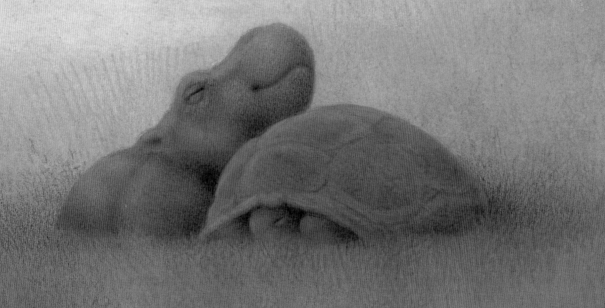

Now Owen and Mzee sleep together.
They swim together.
They eat together.

Whenever Mzee goes for a walk,
moonlight or sunlight, Owen follows
close behind his stubby tail.

Owen's favourite game is still hide-and-seek.

Mzee slips beneath the water, and Owen plunges in
to find him. Mzee nestles in the long grass,
and Owen peers through the grass until he spots him.

Mzee rests behind a rock,
and Owen searches and searches until …

There is Mzee!

And whenever Mzee takes a nap, tucked away inside
his brownish grey – or is it greyish brown? – shell,
Owen waits
and waits
and waits
until he can find Mzee once more.

Then when he finds Mzee, Owen licks his friendly face, lays his head on the tortoise's broad back, and smiles his great pink smile.

Author's Note

The story of Owen and a giant tortoise named Mzee, which means 'old man' in Swahili, is a true one. Owen was rescued by the Kenya Wildlife Service and local fishermen after the hippopotamus and his family were washed down the Sabaki River by a flood and he was brought back to shore by a tsunami wave. Owen was less than a year old – hippopotamus calves ordinarily stay with their mothers for four years – and no one could find his mother. So they brought him to Haller Park, a nature preserve outside of Mombasa. There the lonely young hippo chose Mzee, a 130-year-old male tortoise, to be his mother; and Mzee doesn't seem to mind one little bit.